THE AMERICAN GIRLS

1764 KAYA, an adventurous Nez Perce girl whose deep love for horses and respect for nature nourish her spirit

1774 FELICITY, a spunky, spritely colonial girl, full of energy and independence

1824 JOSEFINA, an Hispanic girl whose heart and hopes are as big as the New Mexico sky

1854  KIRSTEN, a pioneer girl of strength and spirit who settles on the frontier

1864 ADDY, a courageous girl determined to be free in the midst of the Civil War

1904  SAMANTHA, a bright Victorian beauty, an orphan raised by her wealthy grandmother

1934  KIT, a clever, resourceful girl facing the Great Depression with spirit and determination

1944  MOLLY, who schemes and dreams on the home front during World War Two

1944

HAPPY BIRTHDAY,
Molly!

A Springtime Story

BY VALERIE TRIPP

ILLUSTRATIONS NICK BACKES

VIGNETTES KEITH SKEEN

American Girl®

Published by Pleasant Company Publications
For information, address: Book Editor, Pleasant Company Publications,
8400 Fairway Place, P.O. Box 620998, Middleton, WI 53562.

Visit our Web site at **americangirl.com**.

Printed in the China.
05 06 07 08 09 10 11 12 LEO 46 45 44 43 42 41 40

The American Girls Collection®, Molly®, Molly McIntire®, and American Girl®
are registered trademarks of American Girl, LLC.

PICTURE CREDITS
The following individuals and organizations have generously given
permission to reprint images contained in "Looking Back": p. 59—Wisconsin Historical
Society; pp. 60–61—Cal Bernstein, Black Star Publishing Company; Wisconsin Historical
Society WHi(M56)7020; Wisconsin Historical Society WHi(M56)7024; pp. 62–63—Alfred
Eisenstaedt/LIFE Magazine © 1942 Time Inc.; Library of Congress; Wisconsin Historical Society
WHi(X3)43339; from the collection of Anthony J. Evangelista; pp. 64–65—Jane & Michael Stern,
Square Meals, Alfred A. Knopf, New York, © 1984; Magnum Photos, photograph by Wayne Miller;
courtesy Montgomery Ward Catalogue, Fall–Winter 1941–42; Nina Leen/LIFE magazine © 1944
Time Inc.; Wisconsin Historical Society WHi(M56)4506; Luther College Archives, Decorah, Iowa;
Wisconsin Historical Society; courtesy Cindy Stiles.

Cover Background by John Pugh

Library of Congress Cataloging-in-Publication Data

Tripp, Valerie, 1951–
Happy birthday, Molly!: a springtime story
by Valerie Tripp; illustrations, Nick Backes; vignettes, Keith Skeen.
p. cm.—(The American girls collection)
Summary: When an English girl comes to stay at Molly's during
World War II, she and Molly learn to bridge their differences
and ultimately enjoy a wonderful, mutual birthday party.
[1. World War, 1939–1945-United States—Fiction. 2. Friendship—Fiction.]
I. Backes, Nick, ill. II. Title. III. Series.
PZ7.T7363Hap   1989   [Fic]—dc19   89-3904
ISBN 0-937295-90-6
ISBN 0-937295-37-X (pbk.)

TO
EMILY STUART MATTHEWSON

Table of Contents

Molly's Family
and Friends

MOLLY'S FAMILY

DAD
Molly's father, a doctor who is somewhere in England, taking care of wounded soldiers

MOM
Molly's mother, who holds the family together while Dad is away

MOLLY
A nine-year-old who is growing up on the home front in America during World War Two

JILL
Molly's fourteen-year-old sister, who is always trying to act grown-up

RICKY
Molly's twelve-year-old brother—a big pest

BRAD
*Molly's five-year-old
brother—a little pest*

MRS. GILFORD
*The housekeeper, who
rules the roost when
Mom is at work*

EMILY
*An English girl
who comes to stay
with the McIntires*

LINDA
*One of Molly's best
friends, a practical
schemer*

SUSAN
*Molly's other best
friend, a cheerful
dreamer*

GUESS WHAT?

Molly McIntire was skipping rope at the end of her driveway on a blustery afternoon in early spring. She was waiting for her friends Linda and Susan. Molly had a very important piece of news to tell them. Oh, wait until they heard! Molly skipped a little faster, as if that would make them come sooner. The wind sent high white clouds hurrying across the sky. It pushed hard against Molly, too, but she wouldn't budge from her lookout post. Where *were* Linda and Susan? Molly stopped skipping. She shaded her eyes and peered down the street. They were supposed to come over right after lunch. Molly felt as if she had been waiting forever.

At last Molly saw her friends. Linda was walking quickly. She bent into the wind. Her hands were shoved deep in her pockets. She stopped from time to time to wait for Susan, who was much slower. Susan had one foot on the curb and one foot in the gutter, where she was carefully cracking the thin ice over winter's last puddles.

"Hurry up!" Molly called. Linda poked Susan and they both ran to Molly.

"Guess what! Guess what!" shouted Molly as they came near.

"What?" Linda and Susan puffed together.

"An English girl is coming to stay with us!" said Molly happily.

"Oooh!" breathed Susan.

"What do you mean?" asked Linda.

"A girl," said Molly, "from London. Her parents want her to come to America where it's safe. She's supposed to stay with her aunt here in Jefferson until the war's over. But her aunt has pneumonia or something and can't take her, so my mom said she could stay with us."

"Until the war's over?" asked Linda.

"No, just until her aunt gets better," said Molly.

"But Mom said she'd be with us a couple of weeks at least, and that means she'll be here for my birthday."

"Oh, Molly," sighed Susan. "You're so lucky! A real English girl for your birthday!"

"I don't get it," said Linda. "Why is she coming *now?* England has been in the war a long time."

"Well," Molly thought out loud, "maybe her house was just bombed by the Nazis."

"And she's probably raggy and starving like the children in *Life* magazine pictures," added Susan.

Linda shook her head. "Not everybody in England is ragged and starving, Susan," she said. "For all you know, she's as rich as a princess."

"A princess!" said Susan joyfully.

"I bet she even looks like one of the English princesses, Margaret Rose or Elizabeth!" said Molly. "I bet she has dark curly hair and blue eyes. She's going to share my room and come to school with me. She's exactly our age."

the English princesses

"Does she know your dad in England?" asked Linda.

"No, I don't think so," answered Molly.

"When does she come?" asked Susan.

"Today!"

"Today!" shrieked Susan and Linda. "What time?"

"Mom said before dinner," Molly answered.

"Well, I'm not going to stand out here all day waiting for her," said Linda. She was holding her coat collar up around her ears. "I'm cold. Let's go inside."

"Maybe when the English girl is here, Mrs. Gilford will give us little tea sandwiches every afternoon, like they have in England," said Susan dreamily.

"Maybe," said Molly. "Oh, it's going to be so much fun!"

"Will you two come on?" said Linda. She led the way to the house.

The three girls raced inside, through the warm bright kitchen, and down the stairs to the basement. Their new hideaway was in the corner next to Dad's workbench. They had set up a card table there and draped an old blanket over it. It was their pretend bomb shelter. A few Saturdays ago, when they went to the movies, they saw a newsreel that showed

4

the different kinds of bomb shelters people used in England. One bomb shelter was a steel table with sides that

English bomb shelter

rolled down. The sides were made of metal links. The table was set up in a living room. The newsreel showed a family rushing to get under the table at the sound of a warning siren. It seemed almost like a game, the same idea as musical chairs.

The girls had been very impressed. Imagine having a bomb shelter right in your own living room! It was horrifying and exciting at the same time. They had gone straight to Molly's house after the movies and made a pretend bomb shelter of their own. They liked to sit under the blanket-covered table and play that the house was collapsing around them. It was pleasantly scary.

"It smells like mothballs in here," complained Linda as she crawled under the table. "Do we have to have this old blanket over the table all the time?"

"Yes!" said Molly. "Don't you remember the newsreel? When the bombs came the people got under the table and rolled the sides down so they wouldn't get hurt."

"But those sides were like a fence," said Linda. "They had holes so you could at least breathe."

"Well, a blanket is the best we can do," said Molly. "Let's just play."

"Maybe the English girl has a bomb shelter just like this in her house in England," said Susan as she twisted the top off Molly's Girl Scout canteen. They kept the canteen full of water in case they decided to stay in their shelter for a long time. They wanted to keep crackers there, too, but Mrs. Gilford thought cracker crumbs would bring ants.

"Do you think English people ever stay in bomb shelters overnight?" asked Linda. "It's so crowded in here."

"I think sometimes they do," said Molly. She tried to straighten her legs, but there wasn't enough room under the table. "They have to stay in as long as the bombing goes on. Because if they came out too soon, something might fall on them, like bricks or a building or—"

WHAM! Something heavy landed right above their heads. The table wobbled. BAM! The table was struck again.

"Bombs away!" they heard.

The girls looked at each other and giggled, "Ricky!"

Molly lifted the blanket and stuck her head out. Ricky was bouncing his basketball on top of the table. "Don't do that!" Molly said. She didn't mind very much though, because the thud of the basketball made it easy to pretend there were real bombs outside.

"Some bomb shelter," said Ricky. "This wouldn't last two seconds if a real bomb fell. Don't you girls know anything? Real bomb shelters are outside, dug into the ground like caves." He bounced the ball on the table again.

"This is like what they have in England," protested Molly.

"Like fish it is," scoffed Ricky.

"It is, too," said Susan from inside. "We saw it at the movies."

"Where? In the cartoon?" asked Ricky.

"You wait, Ricky," said Molly. "Wait till the English girl comes. She'll tell you about bomb shelters."

Ricky groaned. "Just what I need," he said. "Another dippy girl around." But Molly noticed he didn't say anything more about their bomb shelter.

Ricky had just left when Molly's mother called down the stairs. "Girls? Come up here, please."

"She's here!" squealed Molly. "The English girl!" The three girls tumbled over each other struggling to be the first one out of their bomb shelter. They pounded up the stairs and into the kitchen. Molly stopped so suddenly that Susan stumbled into her back.

There, standing by the kitchen table, was the English girl. Mrs. McIntire was standing behind her, with her hands on the girl's shoulders. "Emily,"

The three girls pounded up the stairs.
There, standing by the kitchen table, was the English girl.

she said, "I'd like you to meet Molly. Molly, this is Emily Bennett." Very gently, she pushed Emily toward Molly. Emily kept her eyes on the floor.

Molly held out her hand and smiled at Emily. "Hi," she said.

Emily glanced up at Molly, then looked down again. She touched Molly's hand with icy fingertips, whispered "How do you do," and stepped backwards toward Mrs. McIntire.

Susan pushed past Molly. "How do you do?" she said. She pulled the sides of her pants legs as if they were the wide skirt of a ball gown and bobbed down in a curtsy. "I'm Susan," she said as she rose awkwardly. "I thought English girls always curtsied."

Ricky snorted and Molly and Linda giggled at Susan. Emily didn't look up, but Molly saw that her ears turned pink with embarrassment. *She thinks we're laughing at her,* Molly thought.

Molly moved toward Emily. "This is Linda," she said. "And here's Ricky, my brother. I have another brother named Brad and a sister named Jill. You'll meet them later."

Everyone was quiet, staring at Emily. Then

Mrs. McIntire said, "We're very glad you're here, Emily. You'll get used to the names and faces soon." She patted her shoulders. "Ricky, would you carry the suitcase upstairs, please? Molly, why don't you show Emily your room." She smiled and said, "It's going to be your room, too, Emily, for as long as you stay with us."

A very quiet parade climbed up the stairs. Ricky was in the lead, with Emily following. Molly, Linda, and Susan lagged behind. Linda whispered to Susan, "She's awfully little. And she sure doesn't look like a princess."

But Susan's eyes were glowing. "Of course she's little. Didn't I tell you she'd be starving?"

Emily was the skinniest girl Molly had ever seen. Her knee socks were twisted and saggy around her legs, which were as thin as spaghetti noodles. Even her hair was skinny. It was gingery-red and absolutely straight, cut short. Her eyes were pale blue. Her skin was pale, too, as if she had not been outside in the sunshine for a very long while.

Ricky put Emily's suitcase on one of the beds in Molly's room and left. Linda and Susan flopped onto the

11

other bed. "Well, here we are," said Molly. "Want me to help you unpack?"

Emily shook her head no. She stood by the door.

"Here," said Molly, "I'll make some room for your stuff in this chest." She scooped up a messy armful of socks from one drawer and shoved them into another. "You can have this whole drawer," she said.

Emily opened her suitcase. Carefully she lined up three pairs of socks, some underwear, and two pairs of pajamas in the drawer.

"Is that all you have?" asked Susan. "Did all your clothes get lost or burned up or something?"

Emily didn't answer. She was hanging two skirts and a white blouse in Molly's closet. She put the blouse on the hanger and buttoned up all the buttons. She folded the collar and moved the shoulders so that they were exactly straight on the bony skeleton of the hanger. "Well, we have lots of clothes and things you can use, so don't worry," Susan added.

Emily put her suitcase under the bed and

smoothed the bedspread. "You sure like things neat," said Molly. She couldn't think of anything else to say. Emily seemed to have a wall around her that made her difficult to talk to. Then Molly thought of something Emily would be familiar with, something she could certainly talk about. "Come on, Emily," she said. "We have something to show you down in the basement."

"Oh, yeah," said Susan. "You'll like this."

Molly led the girls back downstairs. Emily walked stiffly, as if she were cold. When they got to the basement, she moved even more slowly. Molly pointed to the bomb shelter. "See?" she said. "It's a bomb shelter, like you have in England. We play in it all the time." She lifted the edge of the blanket and showed Emily the dark space under the table. "Want to go in?" she asked. "Come on. It's fun."

But Emily backed away from the bomb shelter. "No," she said. "No thank you. I'd rather not." Then she turned and walked quickly back up the stairs.

Molly, Susan, and Linda watched her go. "At least she finally said something," said Linda.

Molly sighed.

"You'd better go up and try to talk to her," said

Susan. "You're supposed to be making friends with her, right?"

"Right," said Molly. She climbed slowly up the stairs to the kitchen. Mrs. McIntire was sweeping the kitchen floor.

"Are you looking for Emily?" she asked. "She said she was going upstairs to write a letter to her parents."

Molly wasn't sure what to do. "Do you think I should go up there?" she asked her mother.

Mrs. McIntire bent over to sweep under the kitchen table. "Nooo," she said. "Why don't you leave Emily in peace for a while. She's probably feeling rather overwhelmed. She's had a big day."

"She's awfully quiet, isn't she?" said Molly. "She never says anything."

Mrs. McIntire straightened and chuckled. "Not everybody is a chatterbox like you are, olly Molly. English children are taught to be reserved—to be very polite and quiet. Emily probably feels shy. Think how you'd feel your first day with a brand new family."

"It seems as if she doesn't like us," said Molly. "She won't smile or anything, and she wouldn't

14

play in the bomb shelter either."

Mrs. McIntire stopped sweeping and thought for a moment. "Give Emily a chance, Molly. Remember, bomb shelters haven't been places for her to play. In fact, the whole world must have seemed cold and dangerous to Emily for a long time. The war in England has been going on since she was five—practically her whole life. I think Emily is like a little crocus who's not sure it's spring yet. It will take some time for her to realize it's safe to come out now." She grinned at Molly. "I imagine quite soon I'll have two chatterboxes on my hands. But meanwhile, you be as warm and friendly and welcoming as you can be to Emily, okay?"

"Okay, Mom," said Molly.

"That's my girl," said Mom.

Mom made it sound easy to make friends with Emily. Molly wasn't sure it would be.

THE BLACKOUT

Molly did her best to make friends with Emily in the next few days, but she didn't get very far. Emily was always polite, but she never seemed to warm up. Molly tried everything. She showed Emily her most treasured possession—her nurse doll, Katharine. Molly's dad had sent Katharine to Molly as a Christmas present. Molly was sure Emily would see that Katharine was the most beautiful doll in the world.

"You see," Molly said as she handed the doll to Emily, "Katharine is dressed like a real English nurse."

"A nurse?" said Emily. "I don't think so."

"What do you mean?" Molly asked. "She comes from England. My dad sent her. And he said she's dressed like the nurses who work in the hospital with him."

Emily straightened Katharine's cap and said politely but firmly, "In England nurses take care of little children. Women who work in hospitals are called sisters. Your doll is dressed like a sister."

"No kidding!" said Molly. "That's great! I've always liked to pretend Katharine is my sister, and now it turns out she really is!"

Emily looked confused. She never understood when Molly said something silly just to be funny. "She isn't *your* sister. She's *a* sister," Emily said.

"Oh, well," said Molly. "Whatever you call her, she's beautiful, isn't she?"

"Very nice," said Emily coolly. She handed the doll back to Molly.

The first day Emily came to school, all the girls asked her lots of questions. They loved her English accent. "She sounds like a movie star, the way she says 'how do you do' and 'rah-ther,'" said Alison Hargate.

All morning long, everyone tried to imitate the

way Emily talked. Emily herself didn't say very much. At lunch, Molly sat next to Emily. She tried to include her in the conversation. During recess, Susan asked, "Was your house ever bombed, Emily?"

Emily said, "No."

Susan kept on. "Did you ever see other houses being bombed?" she asked.

Emily didn't answer right away. Finally, she said, "Yes." Everyone waited for her to say more.

"Well? What was it like?" asked Linda. "Was it exciting?"

Emily looked frosty. "I don't remember," she said.

"Gosh, how could you forget a thing like that?" asked Susan.

Emily shrugged.

There was a chilly silence. Finally, Molly said, "Come on! Let's play jump rope." They all moved into the sunshine.

After a few days, everyone more or less ignored Emily at school. She was so quiet it was an easy thing to do. No one said it, but everyone thought Emily was a disappointment.

"Well, at least she's not a showoff," Linda pointed out. "I was afraid she'd expect all of us to make a fuss over her. I thought she might be stuck-up, but she's not."

"No," sighed Molly. "She's nice enough, I guess. She's just so . . ."

"Quiet," whispered Linda. Everyone giggled.

The girls were walking home from school under trees that were green with new buds. It was one of those tricky spring days that starts as winter in the morning and ends up as summer in the afternoon. Molly had her sweater tied around her waist. Susan had her jacket completely unbuttoned and her arms out of the sleeves. She was only wearing the hood, so the rest flapped behind her like a cape. Linda was the only one still wearing rubbers and a hat.

"Emily even brushes her teeth quietly," said Molly.

"Where is she now?" asked Susan.

"Mom is taking her to see her aunt in the hospital. Then they're going shopping. She has to get some sneakers, only she calls them 'plimsolls.' It's one of her weird English words."

"Plimsolls?" said Linda. She pinched her nose and said in a hoity-toity voice, "Oh, deah! My plimsolls smell simply dreadful."

"I don't think that's very nice, Linda," said Susan. "Did you ever think that maybe Emily is quiet because she doesn't like sounding so different? Or maybe it's because she doesn't know the American words for things. Of course, I still think she's quiet because she's weak and starving. She needs food."

"Mom gives her plenty of food," said Molly. "But she likes strange things like sardines. She doesn't like normal things like cake."

They all tried to imagine not liking cake.

"What kind of cake are you going to have at your birthday party?" asked Susan.

"Mrs. Gilford is going to make that vanilla cake without eggs or butter or milk. She's saved enough sugar rations and chocolate to make frosting," said Molly.

"Yummm," said Susan. "My favorite. If Emily doesn't want her piece, I'll eat it."

"Okay," laughed Molly, "we'll share it."

20

"Talking about cake makes me want some right now," said Susan. "Let's go see if Mrs. Gilford has any."

But Mrs. Gilford said it was too close to dinnertime for any snack other than carrot sticks, so the girls munched their way down to the bomb shelter to play.

Emily and Mrs. McIntire came home just as the rest of the family was sitting down to dinner. "The days are getting longer," Mrs. McIntire said cheerfully. "Spring is here. Doesn't someone in this family have a birthday in the spring?" she asked with a smile.

"I do!" said Molly. "My birthday is only a week away."

"Have you decided what kind of party you want this year?" asked her mother.

"I haven't decided yet," said Molly. "I've been thinking about it and—"

Suddenly, a loud, shrill siren screeched.

"Hurray!" said Ricky. "A blackout!" He jumped up from the table. Emily shrank back in her seat.

"Oh, dear," sighed Mrs. McIntire. "A surprise blackout. All right everyone, let's get going. Jill, you close the blackout curtains. Ricky, turn off all the lights. Molly and Emily, you take Brad downstairs. I'll get some blankets and be right down."

Molly was halfway to the stairs with Brad when she realized Emily wasn't following her. She was sitting at the table, as still as a stone.

"Come on, Emily," said Molly. "Hurry up!"

Emily didn't move.

Molly spoke louder. "Emily, you can't just sit there. It's a blackout. We all have to go downstairs. We have to hurry."

"Don't be scared, Emily," said Brad. "No bombs will come. This is only pretend."

Molly looked hard at Emily. Was Brad right? Was that the problem? Was Emily scared? She certainly looked scared. Her face was white. Molly's voice softened. "It's okay, Emily," she said. "It's just practice, really. I promise."

Emily didn't say anything. But she got up from the table and followed Molly downstairs.

"We have these blackouts every once in a while," Mrs. McIntire said to Emily when everyone was gathered in the basement. "They're a drill for us. There's not much chance of being bombed here, but we want to be ready just in case. So we practice turning out all the lights in town, so no one could see our houses from an airplane. But I imagine you know all about blackouts."

Emily was sitting in the darkest corner of the basement, a little apart from everyone else. Even though it wasn't cold, Emily was wrapped up in a blanket. Molly went over to sit next to her. She couldn't see Emily's face.

"Sometimes they tell us beforehand about the blackouts. Then Mom makes a thermos bottle of hot chocolate . . ." Molly stopped. She saw that Emily was shivering. "Emily? Are you okay?" she asked.

Emily sniffed. Molly realized she was crying. "What's the matter? Are you scared?"

Emily shook her head no. "I hate this," she said suddenly. Molly sat very still and listened. "I hate sitting in the dark, waiting. In England, back during the Blitz, almost every night we had to do this. You'd hear an awful noise, then one split second of silence, and then the explosion." Emily shuddered.

23

"I hate this," Emily said suddenly.
"I hate sitting in the dark, waiting."

"The whole house would shake. If we were on the street when the siren went off, we'd have to make a dash for the tube station—the subway, you call it. We sometimes had to sleep there, with all the other people, all crowded together."

Molly didn't know what to say.

Emily went on. "But it was almost worse afterwards, coming out again. A house you'd walked past every day would be nothing but a pile of stones. Sometimes the flowers would still be growing along a path, and the path would lead to nothing. The house would be gone."

Emily pulled the blanket closer. "In England the bombing isn't exciting at all. It isn't a game. It's terrible. People and . . . things get hurt. They get killed. You Americans don't know."

Molly waited to be sure Emily was finished talking. Then she said, "I guess we really don't know. We're safe here. And now you're safe, too, Emily."

Emily sighed. "But my mum and dad are still there."

Molly moved closer to Emily. She knew how it felt to be worried about someone far away and in danger. "My dad's there, too," she said. "I miss him so much my heart hurts."

Emily looked sideways at Molly. "Sometimes I feel like a coward to have left London."

"Oh, no," said Molly. "I think you're very brave to have been in the bombing. You're as brave as a soldier. You're the bravest person I know, after my dad."

"If I were really brave I would have asked my parents to let me stay," Emily said sadly.

Molly wanted to make Emily feel better. "But . . . but even the princesses of England had to leave London," she said. "I read it in a magazine. They've moved out of the palace in London and out to . . . what's the name of that place?"

"Windsor Castle," said Emily.

"That's right," said Molly. "I read that they sleep in the dungeons every night, to be safe from bombs. They're very brave and they left London. You are just as brave as those princesses, Emily."

Windsor Castle

Emily let the blanket fall away from her head. "Do you like Princess Elizabeth and Princess Margaret Rose, too?" she asked.

"Oh, yes!" said Molly. "I always love to see them in the newsreels and magazines. I think they're so pretty. I even have paper dolls of them."

"You do?" said Emily. Her face looked bright. "I have a scrapbook full of their pictures. I even have pictures of them when they were little girls."

"Ohhh, how wonderful," said Molly. "Did you bring your scrapbook with you?"

"Yes!" said Emily. "It's in my bag, under my bed."

"Could I see it?" Molly asked eagerly.

"Of course!" said Emily.

Just then the all-clear signal blew and the blackout was over. Molly stood up. "Let's go," she said.

Emily gathered the blanket in her arms. "Yes, indeed," she said.

Molly grinned. And Emily actually smiled back.

27

CHAPTER
THREE
—

THE PRINCESSES

"Both the princesses are Girl Guides. That's like your Girl Scouts," Emily was saying. "Here's a picture of them in their uniforms." Molly and Emily were in their room. They were looking at Emily's scrapbook filled with pictures of Princess Elizabeth and Princess Margaret Rose. A clean spring breeze puffed the curtains. Molly was sprawled on the floor on her stomach. Emily was sitting up with her back straight against Molly's bed. Emily always sat up straight. She never sprawled. She never took up too much room. But she wasn't stiff and silent anymore. Spring buds were opening up in the sunshine and Emily was, too.

Emily went on, "Of course, the princesses are practically grown-up ladies now. When they were our age, they used to wear matching clothes like this." She pointed to an old picture of the princesses in matching dresses. They were playing the piano together. A dog was lying asleep at their feet.

"We could do that!" said Molly. She jumped up and flung open the closet door. "We could dress alike, just as the princesses did. We could wear outfits that look like theirs, too. Wouldn't that be fun?"

Emily looked up at Molly. Her eyes were as blue as robins' eggs. Emily didn't say anything, but Molly now knew that when Emily was quiet, it did not mean she didn't care. Emily just didn't say everything she was thinking, the way Molly did when she got excited.

Molly rattled on. "See?" she said. "You have a blue skirt and so do I. That's just the kind of thing the princesses would wear. And we both have white blouses and blue sweaters . . ."

"You could borrow a pair of my blue knee socks," said Emily.

"Okay!" said Molly. "Come on! Let's put these clothes on."

Molly was dressed in a flash. She watched as Emily carefully buttoned her sweater all the way up to her chin. "How come you always button every button?" she asked Emily.

"I keep forgetting how warm your houses are here," said Emily. "In England houses are much colder."

"Even Windsor Castle?" asked Molly.

"Yes," nodded Emily. "Especially castles. The princesses have to make sacrifices because of the war. Their rooms are cold. They can put only a few inches of hot water in the bathtub. They even have to eat dreadful things like parsnips and turnips."

"Turnips!" said Molly. "We have to eat those here!"

Emily smiled. "You see, you're like the princesses, too. Did you ever think that your name starts with M like Margaret Rose—"

"And your name starts with E like Elizabeth," finished Molly.

The girls smiled at each other in the mirror. "Before you came here, I thought you might look like Princess Elizabeth," Molly said to Emily.

Emily grinned. "I rather expected you to look like Shirley Temple, the film star!" she said. "You know, big brown eyes and blond ringlets!"

Molly lifted her braids so that they stuck straight out of her head. "Not exactly blond ringlets. More like long brown sticks," she said.

"I think your hair is very nice, just as it is," said Emily.

"Well, it sure doesn't help me look like a movie star or a princess," sighed Molly. "Of course, if I really wanted to be like one of the princesses, I would have to get a dog. The princesses always have dogs with them, don't they?"

Emily bent over to pull up her knee sock.

"We'll just have to pretend we have dogs," said Molly. She snapped her fingers and said, "Here, boy!" She pretended to pat a dog at her feet. "Good dog!"

Emily looked down at the imaginary dog.

"Let's go for a walk," said Molly. "Don't forget your dog, Em— I mean Elizabeth." She led the way out of the room.

They bumped into Ricky in the hall. When he saw the girls, Ricky smirked. "Why are you two dressed alike?" he said in a disgusted voice. "It makes you look twice as drippy as usual. What stooges!"

Molly put her nose in the air. "Ignore him, Emily," she said. "He only wants attention."

But Emily was staring at the poster Ricky was tacking to his door. It showed fighter planes from different countries. Ricky had cut the pictures out of magazines and labeled them all. "That one's wrong," Emily said quietly.

"What?" said Ricky.

"That plane," said Emily. She pointed to a small picture in the corner. "You've labeled it an enemy plane, but it isn't at all. It's an American plane. I'm sure."

Molly crowed with laughter. "Who's a stooge now, Ricky?" she asked.

"Huh!" said Ricky. He crossed his arms on his chest and looked at Emily. "What does a girl know about fighter planes anyway?"

"Oh, I've seen hundreds of fighter planes flying over England," said Emily.

"You have?" asked Ricky. He had never seen even one.

"Of course," Emily said patiently. "Look here. See these white bands over the nose and the tail? That's what tells you it's an American plane. Besides—" she squinted at the blurry picture—"if you look very hard, you can tell that's a star, not a swastika, there near the tail. All the American planes have stars on them."

"I know *that*," snapped Ricky. He frowned at the poster and started to take it down. Without turning around he said, "Do you see any other mistakes?"

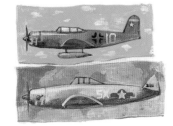

"Not right off," Emily said airily. "I'll look more carefully later though. Molly and I are going for a walk now." She and Molly floated down the hall, down the stairs, and outside.

It had rained during the night, and the girls had to skirt around mud puddles as they strolled along dragging their jump ropes. They were using the jump ropes as leashes for their imaginary dogs.

Molly had a fine time pretending her dog was frisky.

"No, no!" she said. "Don't go in that puddle! Bad dog!" Molly yanked her jump rope through the water. Then she pretended to trip. She giggled, "Ooops! My dog twisted the leash around my legs! This is fun, isn't it?"

"Mmmhmm," Emily answered in her usual soft-spoken way. Her dog seemed to be well-behaved and as quiet as Emily was herself.

"Of course, it would be better if we had real dogs," said Molly. "Do you like dogs, Emily?"

Emily's eyes were shining. "Oh, yes," she said. "I love dogs."

"Me, too," said Molly. "I think puppies are cute. And dogs are so much fun to play with."

"Yes," said Emily.

"Even before I was a princess, I wished I had a dog," Molly went on. "A dog can really be your friend. Don't you think so?"

But Emily didn't answer. Her imaginary dog must have tugged on its leash because Emily quickly moved a few steps ahead of Molly.

During the next few days, Molly and Emily took their imaginary dogs for a walk every afternoon. Everyone in the family got used to seeing them in their matching princess outfits, dragging their jump rope leashes and playing with their invisible dogs. The two girls liked to share Molly's roller skates, each wearing one, and skate down the sidewalk pretending their dogs were running behind.

"It's too bad we can't get a pair of skates for you," said Molly to Emily one afternoon. "But they're not making skates because of the war."

"Oh, I don't mind," said Emily cheerfully. "Remember, we're princesses, and princesses never complain about the sacrifices they have to make."

Molly joked, "I wonder if the princesses ever skated with their dogs? I bet there's lots of room to skate in Windsor Castle."

They giggled as they skated up the driveway.

Mrs. McIntire was kneeling in the flower garden. She was pulling dead leaves away from some daffodils that were beginning to bloom. "Hello, your highnesses," she said. "What's all the giggling about?"

"We were thinking about skating in a palace," said Molly.

"I wish you would think about what kind of birthday party you'd like to have. It's less than a week away, you know," Mrs. McIntire said to Molly.

"I know," said Molly. "I just can't decide. I was thinking of going to the movies, but we did that last year. I want to do something different."

"How do you celebrate birthdays, Emily?" Mrs. McIntire asked.

Emily thought a moment. "In England, we used to have a tea party and—"

"A tea party!" Molly broke in. "Oooh! That's perfect! Can we do that, Mom?"

"I don't see why not," said Mrs. McIntire. "Emily can tell us exactly what to do."

Emily glowed. "Of course, I haven't actually had a big birthday party in a long time. Not since

"Hello, your highnesses," said Mom.
"And how are your imaginary dogs?"

the war started, really, because it's impossible to get sweets and special foods," she added quickly. "But when I was much younger, I had a party with ten girls. The room was decorated with flowers and ribbons, and we played games and ate lovely treats."

"Like princesses!" said Molly. "That's what my birthday party will be: the princesses' tea party!" Then Molly had a wonderful idea. "Emily, why don't you share my birthday with me? It will make up for the parties you've missed. We'll have a tea party, and we'll be the princesses, you and me. We'll dress up so we'll look alike and everything. It will be the most wonderful birthday party anyone ever had. What do you think?"

Emily's cheeks were as pink as posies. "I think it would be very nice indeed," she said.

Molly knew that was an excited answer, coming from Emily. Emily must be very, very pleased, just as pleased as Molly was herself.

PLANNING THE PARTY

The very next day, Molly and Emily wrote out the invitations to their shared birthday party. Emily showed Molly the proper way to word the invitations.

"You see," Emily said, "in England we do invitations like this." Emily pushed her wispy hair behind her ears, hunched over the paper and wrote

*Mrs. James McIntire requests
the honour of your presence at a tea
to celebrate the birthdays of
Miss Molly McIntire   Miss Emily Bennett
Saturday, the twenty-second of April
four o'clock at her home*

"That's wonderful!" said Molly. "It's so . . . so English."

Emily smiled.

"The only thing is, I'm a little worried because I don't think any of my friends really drink tea," said Molly. "So probably we should have cocoa instead."

Emily said slowly, "In England it's always real tea. I suppose you could put lots of hot milk and honey in the tea, so that your friends will like it."

"I guess so," said Molly. "Usually at birthday parties we have cold milk with peanut butter sandwiches or hot dogs. Of course, at Alison Hargate's party we had ginger ale."

Emily shook her head. "In England we have tea sandwiches, not peanut butter or hot dogs. Tea sandwiches are very thin, not like American sandwiches. And the crusts are cut off."

"Well, that sounds okay," said Molly. "What's in the sandwiches?"

"Meat paste or watercress," said Emily.

"Meat paste?" asked Molly. "What's that?"

Emily explained. "It's a paste sort of like peanut butter, only it's made out of ground-up meat.

Maybe ham or liver."

"Liver?" said Molly, horrified. "I don't think my friends will like that."

Emily sighed. "I suppose we could have just bread and butter . . ."

"Butter is rationed," said Molly. "It will have to be bread and margarine."

"Very well," said Emily.

"Anyway," said Molly, "everyone mostly just eats the ice cream and cake at a birthday party."

"In England we don't have ice cream at tea," said Emily.

"No ice cream? Not even when it's a birthday tea party? You just have plain old cake?" Molly asked.

"Oh, no, indeed!" said Emily. "Not *plain* cake. At a tea party you'd have something special. Let's see," she thought. "It's not proper to have treacle pudding at tea. You'd have little cakes or a tart. Yes, I think probably a tart. A lemon tart."

"Wait a minute," said Molly. She wasn't absolutely sure what a lemon tart was, but she didn't like the sound of it. "Are you saying we'll have a lemon tart instead of a regular cake?"

Emily said, "Yes."

"But—but what do you put the candles in?" sputtered Molly. "And what do you write Happy Birthday on?"

Emily didn't answer.

"Listen, Emily," said Molly. "My very favorite birthday thing, I mean what I myself like the best, is a big layer cake. It's not a birthday without a cake. And Mrs. Gilford has even saved enough of our cocoa ration for chocolate frosting this year. I know you'll like it." Emily didn't say anything, so Molly went on, "Maybe we could make the cake look English. We could make it in the shape of a castle or something . . ." Her voice trailed off. The two girls sat in stony silence.

At last Molly said, "What if we have an American cake, but all the rest of the food is English?"

"Then it wouldn't be a proper English princesses' tea at all," said Emily.

"Yes, it would," said Molly.

"No," said Emily briskly, "it would not."

"Okay, okay," said Molly. "As long as you're sure that's what the princesses would have."

"Oh, yes," said Emily. "I'm sure."

"Then let's go tell Mom about the food," Molly said to Emily. But to herself she said, *Margarine sandwiches, milky tea, and a lemon tart. Maybe this tea party was not such a hot idea after all.*

But all the girls at school thought the tea party sounded absolutely wonderful. All week long, while they were playing jump rope and dodgeball and hopscotch in the fresh spring sunshine, all anyone talked about was "Emily's tea party."

"How simply elegant!" gushed Susan. "It's so

grown-up! I've never had real tea before!"

"You are so lucky, Molly," said Alison Hargate. "Emily can tell you just how everything is done in England."

Everyone envied Molly so much, she began to think she really must be lucky. No one else seemed to think a lemon tart was so bad.

★

By the night before the party, Molly and Emily both felt jittery with excitement as they blew up balloons and made party hats.

"Hey, Emily," said Molly. "We'd better not forget to make crowns for ourselves."

"Crowns?" asked Emily.

"Sure, so everyone will know we're the princesses," said Molly. "I think I have two long dress-up dresses we can wear."

Emily laughed softly. "Oh, Molly, you're thinking of fairy tale princesses. Princess Elizabeth and Princess Margaret Rose wear normal clothes."

"But I've seen pictures of them in crowns and long dresses," said Molly stubbornly. "Remember? There's a picture like that in your scrapbook."

"That picture was taken when their father was crowned the King of England," said Emily. "They don't wear those clothes for a tea party."

"Oh," said Molly. She had imagined herself curtsying deep into a billow of skirt. "Well, at least I have a nice party dress from last year."

"In fact, since it's a wartime party, the princesses would probably wear skirts and jumpers—you call them sweaters," said Emily. "They'd dress just as usual."

This was too much. "I'm not wearing boring old school clothes to my birthday party," Molly stated flatly. "All the other girls will have on their party dresses."

"The princesses—" Emily began.

"I don't care," said Molly. "I'm going to wear my party dress and that's final."

"But then we won't look like the princesses," said Emily.

"Too bad," said Molly.

"But then we won't look the *same*," said Emily.

All of a sudden, Molly realized that Emily didn't *have* a party dress. She squirmed. No wonder Emily wanted them to wear skirts and sweaters. Molly felt sorry for Emily just then. "Oh, all right," she said. "We'll wear regular clothes so we'll look like the princesses."

The girls went back to decorating. They put poppers, candy cups, and blow outs at each place on the table. They hung crepe paper streamers across the ceiling. The room began to look ready for a wonderful party. Through the doors to the living room, the girls could hear a radio show beginning. Molly sang along to the music. "My country 'tis of thee . . ." She heard Emily singing softly to the same tune. Emily was singing, "God save our noble king . . ."

"That's an American song," said Molly. "The words are 'My country 'tis of thee.'"

"No, the words are 'God save our noble king,'" said Emily. "It's a British song."

"It is not!" said Molly.

"It is, too!" said Emily. "It's our national anthem!"

"Well, it's an American song now," said Molly.

"It was a British song first," said Emily. "You Americans think everything in the world belongs to you."

"We do not!" said Molly.

"Would you two cut it out?" said Ricky. "I want to listen to this program."

Molly and Emily were quiet. Molly felt as if the heat were turned on too high in the room. She took off her sweater and tossed it on the floor.

"Molly, please," said Mrs. McIntire. "Don't throw your clothes around like that. Can't you take care of your things properly, the way Emily does?"

Molly grabbed her sweater and flung it on a chair. The voice from the radio was the only one in the room. "Battle-weary Britons welcomed more American soldiers today. They call our boys 'the Yanks.' The Yanks bring hope to these tired English people. Everyone knows it's up to these Yanks to save England and the world from Hitler's threat . . ."

"Oh!" said Emily suddenly. "That's not true!"

Everyone was startled. They looked at Emily. Her face was red. "I'm so tired of hearing how America is winning the war when England has been fighting ever so much longer."

"But it's true," said Molly. "England can't win the war without America. Our soldiers are stronger than yours."

"Oh, you Americans!" said Emily. "You always have everything your own way. You think you are so important!"

"We are important," Molly began.

But Mrs. McIntire interrupted. "Girls!" she said. "England and America are allies, remember? We're fighting together." She shook her head at the girls. "I think you are both overtired and overexcited about this party. You two princesses take your imaginary dogs and go upstairs to bed. I'll come up to tuck you in later."

Molly and Emily stalked out of the room, too angry to look at each other. Molly kept thinking about her party while she got ready for bed. Well, it was supposed to be her party. Now it was "Emily's tea party." Molly threw a candy cup onto the floor.

"Don't!" said Emily. "You'll ruin it."

"Who cares?" said Molly. "Everything is already ruined and you ruined it. You and your dumb old tea party. I don't want milky tea and lemon tarts! I don't want to wear ugly old clothes!"

"Food and clothes! That's all you ever worry about, nothing important," said Emily. "You don't know anything about what the war is really like.

"Everything is already ruined," said Molly,
"and you ruined it."

You don't even know what's real. You think the princesses are out of a fairy tale, you pretend you have a dog, and you make a game out of bombing. You're just a spoiled child who has to have everything her own way."

"Spoiled!" said Molly. "I was going to let you share my whole birthday! Now I don't even want you at the party. I let you talk me into doing everything the way you do it in England. In England! I'm so tired of hearing that! If it's so great in England why don't you just go back there?"

Emily pulled the covers over her head. Molly thought she heard some sniffles, but she was too mad to care. *I gave in and gave in and gave in to Emily,* she thought. *I'm not giving in anymore. Tomorrow I'll tell Mom we're having a regular American birthday party and Emily's not invited.* And with that thought, Molly pulled the covers over her head and tried to go to sleep.

YANK AND BENNETT

Usually Molly woke up early and happy on her birthday. But this birthday morning, the dark words she and Emily had said the night before put a shadow on the day. Outside it was gray and cloudy. A cold drizzle was falling. It certainly didn't look like a happy birthday, and Molly didn't feel happy either. She felt bad about the mean things she had said to Emily. She had started by saying she didn't want a lemon tart at the party and ended by saying she didn't want Emily at the party. How did everything get so mixed up?

Molly looked over at Emily's bed. It was empty, perfectly made as usual. Emily was in the bathroom, washing her face. When she came back and saw Molly was awake, she looked away hurriedly. Molly thought Emily looked sorry, too.

Molly tried to think what Dad would do. It was at times like this that she realized how much she needed Dad. Molly looked at Emily's back. One thing was sure. Dad would say that no party was half as important as a friend's feelings. Molly swallowed hard. "Emily . . ." she began.

Emily looked around her shoulder at Molly. At that moment, the door swung open and Mom and Brad burst in. "Happy birthday!" they shouted. "Happy birthday, Molly! Happy birthday, Emily!"

Mom gave both girls a big hug. "Jill! Ricky!" she called. "You can come in now."

Jill and Ricky walked slowly into the room. They were each holding something in their arms. Molly sat up straight in her bed.

"Puppies!" Molly cried. "Puppies! Oh, they're perfect!"

Jill put one puppy on Molly's bed. Ricky put the other puppy into Emily's arms. "We thought you two princesses deserved real puppies," said Mrs. McIntire.

"Yeah, so you can stop acting like nuts, talking to dogs that aren't there," said Ricky.

Everyone laughed and Molly said, "Thank you! A real puppy! It's too good to be true!" She scooped up her puppy and gave it a kiss. "I love it."

Emily looked at Mrs. McIntire. "Thank you," she said.

Mrs. McIntire smiled. "We'll leave your highnesses to get acquainted with your puppies," she said. "Meanwhile, the rest of us will go make a royal breakfast for you."

Molly's puppy snuggled closer to her chest. It was fat and warm and had snappy brown eyes and pointed ears. Its four little feet were white, as if it had wandered into a puddle of paint by mistake. And it had gingery-red spots, exactly the color of Emily's hair. Molly hugged the puppy. It reached up and licked her under the chin.

"Emily! Emily! Look!" said Molly. "Mine's licking me!"

Emily was cuddling her puppy, too. She rubbed her cheek against its head and murmured. Molly heard her say, "It's been so long."

"What do you mean, 'so long'?" asked Molly.

Emily put her puppy in her lap. She stroked its head. "I used to have a dog," she said. "I didn't tell you before because . . ." Emily paused. "Because my dog was killed. It was one year ago. My dog was trapped under a building that was hit by a bomb."

Molly held her puppy even closer. "Oh, Emily," she said. "That's horrible. I'm so sorry. I'm really, really sorry." Molly brought her puppy over to Emily's bed. The puppies began to play together.

"You know, Emily," Molly went on, "I think you were right about some of the things you said last night. The war has been harder for you. It hasn't been as real for me."

Emily looked at Molly. "I wasn't completely right," she said. "I realized something when I was feeling so bad last night. First I thought about how much I miss my parents. Then I thought, I've only been away from them for a few weeks. Your father has been away from you for two years. I know you miss him very much. The war is hard for you, too, Molly."

Molly nodded. Emily's puppy had the sash of her bathrobe in its mouth. The puppy growled as it tugged and yanked on the sash. Emily and Molly

*"I'm going to call my puppy Bennett,
after my good English friend," said Molly.*

laughed. "Your puppy is a tough little fighter," Molly said. "What are you going to name it?"

"I think I'll call my puppy Yank," said Emily. "Because it's a good American dog."

"I'm going to call my puppy Bennett, after my good English friend," said Molly.

The girls smiled at each other. "Wait till everyone at the party sees our puppies," said Molly. "They'll know we're *really* the princesses." She grinned at Emily. "Even if we don't have crowns and long dresses."

The door opened and Mrs. McIntire stuck her head in. She smiled at the girls, then pretended to scold. "If you princesses weren't such lazybones, lying around in your pajamas all day, you would have found another birthday surprise in your closet by now."

Molly jumped up and opened the closet door. There, side by side, were two white pinafore dresses trimmed with ruffles. The dresses were beautiful. They were absolutely alike. There was one for Molly and one for Emily.

Emily gasped, "They're lovely."

Molly ran over and gave her mother a hug.

"Oh, Mom!" she said. "Now everything is perfect. Thank you!"

"Thank you very much *indeed*," said Emily.

"You're very welcome, both of you," said Mrs. McIntire. "Now put on your play clothes and come have breakfast. You have a lot to do before your birthday tea party."

Emily picked up her puppy and smiled at Molly. "I think this is a very happy birthday," she said.

Molly smiled back. "Very happy *indeed*."

LOOKING BACK

GROWING UP
IN
1944

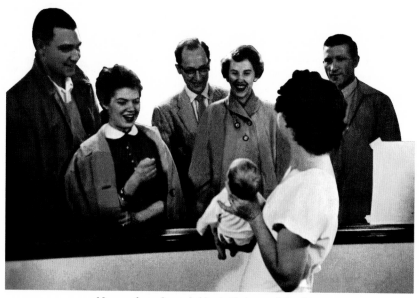
Nurses showed new babies to their proud families.

When girls like Molly were growing up, most
babies were born in hospitals. Hospitals didn't allow
mothers and fathers to be together for the birth of a
baby. Instead, a mother went to the delivery room and
a father stayed in the waiting room. New babies spent
most of their time in the hospital nursery. Their fathers,
grandparents, and other adults could watch them there
through a glass window. But their brothers and sisters
didn't come to visit because in the 1940s, children
weren't allowed in hospitals unless they were sick.

New babies and their mothers usually went home
from the hospital after about a week. Sometimes a

practical nurse was hired to go home with them, because taking care of a new baby was lots of work. Most babies were fed *formula* that had to be made from milk, sweetener, and water. They drank from glass bottles with nipples that had to be sterilized in boiling water.

Premixed, canned baby formula was new in the 1940s.

But in some ways it was easier to take care of babies in the 1940s than it had ever been before. There was canned baby food, and since most American homes had washing machines it wasn't very hard to keep the baby's diapers and clothes clean. Still, clothes driers had not been invented, so there was a lot of wash to hang out on the line to dry.

Most children grew up healthy in the 1940s because shots called *vaccinations* kept them from getting serious diseases like smallpox. When children got sick with measles or chicken pox, they stayed at home and their parents hung warning signs outside the house. The signs told everyone to stay away until the sick person was better. This kept diseases from spreading.

Vaccinations helped keep children healthy in the 1940s.

Children growing up in the 1940s didn't worry much about being sick, but they had to face something that was much worse. Most of the world was fighting in World War Two. Since nearly all of the battles happened far away from the United States, American children were safe. But other children in the world were in danger because of the fighting. Some children were *evacuated*—taken out of their own countries and brought to the United States so that they could be safe, too.

Because of the war, American factories spent more time making equipment for fighting than making things like toys. Toys became costly treats that were hard to get, so children like Molly often had

In England, families had bomb shelters in their basements.

to invent their own playthings. They used sticks, tin cans, or clotheslines to play games like stickball, kick-the-can, or jump rope. But children like Molly didn't spend all their time playing. They did chores like making their beds, helping with dishes,

There were no dishwashers in the 1940s.

and taking out the garbage. They often got allowances of ten or fifteen cents a week for doing these chores. They spent their allowances on things like comic books and tickets to the movies.

Children enjoyed books like the Nancy Drew and Hardy Boys mysteries. And everyone loved to listen to the radio. Children like Molly tuned in to their favorite radio programs just as boys and girls today watch their favorite TV shows. Radio programs about characters like The Lone Ranger, Buck Rogers, and Captain Midnight were especially popular. Kids often sent away for free toys decorated with pictures of their favorite radio show characters.

Kids sent away for free toys they heard about on the radio.

A birthday party was just as important in the 1940s as it is today. However, parties were much simpler then. Most children had their parties at home, with home-made decorations and food. Birthday cakes, ice cream, and candy were all special treats because sugar was in short supply. At parties, children wore dressy clothes and played simple games. An apple or a handful of peanuts might be the prize for winning a game.

By the time girls like Molly turned thirteen, they thought of themselves as *teenagers*. During the 1940s, people began to see that the teenage years were a special stage of life and that teen-agers had their own special interests.

Teenagers danced the jitterbug.

Teenagers listened to records in stores more often than they bought them.

For the first time, fashions were created just for teenagers. Teenagers listened to their own music, read their own magazines, and spent time at their own "hangouts." Teenage boys earned money by delivering newspapers and working in soda fountains. Teenage girls made money by baby-sitting for mothers who were working at war jobs. Teenagers learned how to drive cars and could go out on dates without adults being with them.

Teenagers learned to drive.

By the time a girl like Molly graduated from high school, her teenage years were over and she was expected to be a grownup. She had many choices to make. She could go to college, get a job, or get married. Sometimes she did all three.

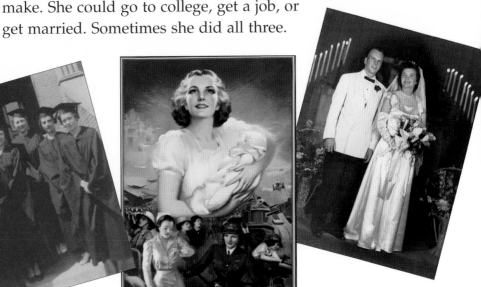

A Sneak Peek at

Molly

Saves the Day

*Molly's having a great time at summer camp—
until the campers go to war!*

The next morning, every camper put on a red armband or a blue armband to show which team she was on. Right after breakfast, the Red Team left the Dining Hall with the flag. Molly and Susan watched Linda march down the path toward the Red canoes with the rest of her team. They looked like an army, parading two by two like soldiers, carrying their bag lunches, and singing,

> "We are the Reds,
> Mighty, mighty Reds.
> Everywhere we go-oh,
> People want to know-oh,
> Who we are.
> So we tell them:
> We are the Reds,
> Mighty, mighty Reds . . ."

Linda turned around and rolled her eyes at Molly. Molly grinned. She remembered what Linda had said last night about not taking Color War too seriously. *I should be more like Linda*, Molly thought. But she snapped to attention when Dorinda said in her bossiest voice, "Blue Army report to HQ on the double."

"HQ?" Susan asked Molly. "Who's that?"

"It's not a person, it's a place," said Molly. "HQ stands for headquarters. I think she means the boathouse. Let's go."

Molly and Susan followed the rest of the Blue Army to the boathouse. Two girls stood as guards at the door in case the Red Army had left spies behind. When she got the signal that the coast was clear, Dorinda began.

She frowned at the girls. "We are going to win this Color War," she said sternly. "And the only way to win is to fight as hard as we can. Do you understand?"

Everyone mumbled, "Yes."

"All right," Dorinda went on. "Here is the plan of attack. The flag is on Chocolate Drop Island. To get it, we obviously have to canoe across the lake. You will each be assigned a buddy. You and your buddy will paddle a canoe together. We will load up and begin the attack at oh-nine-hundred."

"Oh-nine-hundred?" Susan whispered to Molly. "Where's that?"

"It's not a place, it's a time," said Molly. "It's the army way to say nine o'clock."

"Well, why doesn't she just say nine o'clock?" asked Susan. "We're a team. We're not *really* an army."

Molly put a finger to her lips. Dorinda was scowling at her and at Susan.

"Pay attention, troops!" Dorinda ordered. She turned and uncovered a big map of Camp Gowonagin tacked to the wall.

Everyone said, "Oooh." The map looked as if it had been very carefully drawn. Molly realized Dorinda and her helpers must have been up all night making it. Molly's heart sank. Under Dorinda's command, Color War seemed less and less like a game among friends and more and more like a war between enemies.

The map showed the boathouse, the lake, and Chocolate Drop Island. Dorinda used a long stick to point to places on the map as she talked.

First, she pointed to the boathouse. "We will set out from here," she said. Then she pointed to a place on the far side of Chocolate Drop Island labeled "Beach." "We will land here. From

the beach we will march up Chocolate Drop Hill.
vI will capture the flag. The rest of you will take the
Red Army prisoner. You will lead the prisoners back
to your canoes and return them to our HQ. I will
meet you here no later than ten-hundred."

"She means ten o'clock, right?" Susan asked
Molly.

But Molly wasn't listening to Susan. There was
something she didn't understand. It wasn't the plan.
She understood the plan perfectly. The plan was easy.
In fact, it was too easy, much too easy. Timidly, Molly
raised her hand. Everyone turned around and stared
at her.

"Yes?" snapped Dorinda.

Molly stood up. She clasped her hands behind
her back. "Uh, I get the plan," she said. "I know what
we're supposed to do. But I wonder what they're
going to do. The Red Army, I mean. Won't they have
scouts who will see us coming across the lake? The
lake isn't very wide there."

"How do *you* think we should cross the lake?"
Dorinda asked sharply. "Should we swim underwater?"

Molly's hands were clammy. Everyone at camp

71

*"How do **you** think we should cross the lake?"*
Dorinda asked sharply. "Should we swim underwater?"

knew she hated to swim underwater. She wanted
to sit down, but she made herself speak up. "I just
think the Red Army will be waiting for us at the
beach when we land. They'll be ready to take all
of us prisoner. Isn't there any place we could land
where they wouldn't see us?"

"No," said Dorinda. "Those are my orders."

"But," Molly started to say, "but what if—"

Dorinda crossed her arms over her chest and
said, "If you are too chicken to do this you can stay
behind. Be a deserter. Otherwise, go with your
friend Susan. The two of you can be buddies and
bring up the rear in your canoe. That way the rest
of us can protect you."

Molly sat down, shamed into quiet. She
pretended to straighten her blue armband.

"Now, go to the canoes! The rest of the buddy
assignments will be made there," said Dorinda.
Everyone filed out of the boathouse. No one would
look at Molly.

READ ALL OF MOLLY'S STORIES,
available at bookstores and *www.americangirl.com.*

MEET MOLLY • An American Girl
While her father is fighting in World War Two,
Molly and her brother start their own war at home.

MOLLY LEARNS A LESSON • A School Story
Molly and her friends plan a secret project to help the
war effort, and learn about allies and cooperation.

MOLLY'S SURPRISE • A Christmas Story
Molly makes plans for Christmas surprises,
but she ends up being surprised herself.

HAPPY BIRTHDAY, MOLLY! • A Springtime Story
An English girl comes to stay with Molly,
but she's not what Molly expects!

MOLLY SAVES THE DAY • A Summer Story
At summer camp, Molly has to pretend to be her
friend's enemy and face her own fears, too.

CHANGES FOR MOLLY • A Winter Story
Dad will return from the war any day! Will he arrive in time
to see the "grown-up" Molly perform as Miss Victory?

◆

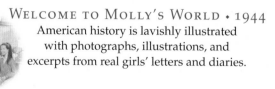

WELCOME TO MOLLY'S WORLD • 1944
American history is lavishly illustrated
with photographs, illustrations, and
excerpts from real girls' letters and diaries.

MORE TO DISCOVER! While books are the heart of

The American Girls Collection® they are only the beginning. The stories

in the Collection come to life when you act them out with the beautiful American Girls dolls and their exquisite clothes and accessories. To request a free catalogue full of things girls love, send in this postcard, call **1-800-845-0005,** or visit our Web site at **americangirl.com**.

Please send me an American Girl®catalogue.

My name is _____

My address is _____

City _____ State _____ Zip _____

1961i

My birth date is ____/____/____ E-mail address _____
month   day   year *Fill in to receive updates and web-exclusive offers.*

Parent's signature _____

And send a catalogue to my friend.

My friend's name is _____

Address _____

City _____ State _____ Zip _____

1225i

If the postcard has already been removed from this book
and you would like to receive an American Girl® catalogue,
please send your name and address to:

American Girl
P.O. Box 620497
Middleton, WI 53562-0497

You may also call our toll-free number, **1-800-845-0005,**
or visit our Web site at **americangirl.com**.

‖ ‖

Place
Stamp
Here

PO BOX 620497
MIDDLETON WI 53562-0497

|ₗ|ₗ|ₗₗₗ|ₗₗ|ₗ|ₗ|ₗₗ||ₗₗₗₗₗ|ₗₗ||||ₗₗₗₗₗₗ|ₗₗ||ₗₗₗₗ|ₗₗₗₗₗₗₗ||ₗₗₗₗₗₗ|ₗₗₗ|ₗₗ||ₗ|